DERANGED

DERANGED

Why was this happening to her?

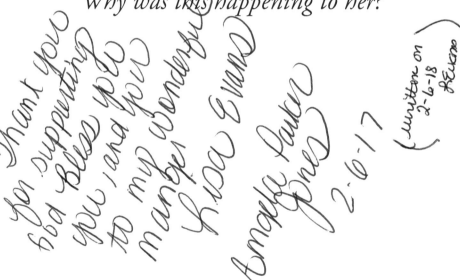

Thank you
for supporting
you, and you
Bless you
to my wonderful
nantes
Rida Evans
Angela Parker
Jones
2-6-17
(written on
2-6-18
Second)

ANGELA PARKER JONES

Library of Congress Control Number:		2017911132
ISBN:	Hardcover	978-1-5434-3699-0
	Softcover	978-1-5434-3698-3
	eBook	978-1-5434-3697-6

Print information available on the last page.

Rev. date: 07/14/2017

To order additional copies of this book, contact:
Xlibris
1-888-795-4274
www.Xlibris.com
Orders@Xlibris.com
764013

I want to first give a Honor to God...

Secondly, a special thanks to my

husband Christopher Jones, my

two daughters NaKeeda Parker and

Destinee Highsmith... I love you...

"HELP ME!" KINSEY screamed, running from her house with blood dripping from her clothes. As Kinsey was falling to the ground, she looked back, and a man was standing on her front porch, staring at her. She got up from the ground and continued to run to the neighbor's house.

"Help me! Please help me!" She banged on the door.

Her neighbor Sarah opened her door. "Oh my!" she said. "What happened to you?" Sarah grabbed Kinsey. "Come in!"

Kinsey went in, crying and gasping for air. "Can you please call the police?"

Sarah said, "What happened to you?"

Kinsey said, "I was asleep, and a man broke into my house. He came into my room and tried to kill me! He stabbed me in my arm and leg. He dragged me into the living room. I saw the front door was left open, and somehow, I managed to get away.

"As I tried to run, I looked back and saw the man standing on my front porch, watching me run away and falling to ground. He never said a word. I couldn't run very fast because of my wounds, but he never even tried to run after me. He never said a word. Please call the police now before he gets away!"

Sarah called 911; she reported the incident. The police came twenty minutes after the call.

When Kinsey heard the sirens getting louder, she went back to her house. Two police officers —Sergeant Peter and Sergeant Pamala.

They both got out of the police car quickly. "Ms. Kinsey?"

"Yes, I am she," Kinsey responded.

"Do you need medical attention for your arm and leg?" Sergeant Pamala asked.

"No, I am fine," Kinsey said, holding her arm.

Angela Parker Jones

"We need to look around your home inside and out," Sergeant Peter said. He began creeping around with the gun upright from room to room. Sergeant Pamala took pictures and gathered evidence in the home.

She saw blood on the floor that came from Kinsey. She scooped samples of blood and placed them in her evidence kit. Sergeant Peter was looking around outside with his gun and flashlight. He walked from one end of Kinsey's house to the other.

Sergeant Peter opened Kinsey's shed very slowly. "Is there anyone in here?" he shouted, slowly stepping into the shed. It was very dark and crowded with boxes and tools. *Why would a woman have such a large collection of tools?* Sergeant Peter thought to himself. After he searched the shed from top to bottom, he found nothing and no one.

After about thirty minutes of looking inside of Kinsey's house, garage, backyard, and shed, Sergeant Peter and Sergeant Pamala didn't find a trace of anything but Kinsey's blood.

Angela Parker Jones

"Did you find anything?" Sergeant Peter asked Sergeant Pamala.

"I only took samples of blood. It's most likely Kinsey's blood, but I will take it in to be sure. What about you, Sergeant?" Pamala said, putting her evidence kit in the trunk of her car.

"No, I didn't see anything!" Sergeant Peter said with a puzzled face. "I didn't even see footprints."

"Yeah, that is pretty strange," Sergeant Pamala said. "We're dealing with a clever man."

After Sergeant Peter and Pamala typed up their reports, they both went back inside to talk to Kinsey.

"Ms. Kinsey!"

No answer.

"Ms. Kinsey!"

"Yes? I'm here," Kinsey said, coming out of her kitchen.

"We want to say that we are sorry. There are no signs that anyone has been here, but we will do a further investigation," Sergeant Peter said.

"He was here, I promise! Look at me!" Kinsey screamed and cried.

"We aren't saying that he wasn't, Ms. Kinsey. All we're saying is that he cleaned up after himself really well," Sergeant Pamala explained to Kinsey.

"What am I supposed to do? What if he comes back?"

"We will do all that we can to find this man, but until then, do you have a relative that you can stay with until everything calms down?" Sergeant Peter asked.

"No, I don't," Kinsey said, sitting down on her sofa.

"We will have a police officer in this area every hour for your safety," Sergeant Peter said, taking notes on his small pad.

"I will feel comfortable with that," Kinsey said.

"We're truly sorry for everything that happened to you tonight. Try to get some rest, and if you hear or see anything else unusual, please call us," Sergeant Pamala said, handing

Angela Parker Jones

Kinsey a card with both her and Sergeant Peter's numbers on it.

"Okay," Kinsey said with teary eyes. "Thank you, both."

"Have a good night, Ms. Kinsey, and be safe." Both Sergeant Pamala and Peter said before Kinsey shut and locked the door behind them.

By the time Kinsey finished cleaning herself up and making a cup of hot tea, it was 2:00 a.m. She could not go back to sleep with the way she felt, so she sat down on her living room couch, just staring at a painting she did a few years ago. The painting was of a man and a woman holding hands on the beach.

Ring, ring, ring!

Kinsey picked up the telephone.

"Hello, Kinsey? Hey, I'm calling to make sure you are okay," Sarah said, sounding worried.

"I'm okay. I'm a little frightened, but I'll be okay." Kinsey smiled a little. "Thank you for checking on me."

"That is great. I'm just down the street if you need me. Get some rest, Kinsey, and I will call you later."

They both ended the call. Kinsey stayed up for hours, replaying the incident that happened earlier that night. Time passed, and she dosed off.

Around 4:00 a.m., someone banged on her door. *Boom! Boom! Boom!* Kinsey got up and went to the door to look through the peephole. She didn't see anyone.

"Is anyone there?" said Kinsey. She waited for an answer. No one responded.

She began looking out her windows. She saw nothing. Kinsey cut off her lights except for one lamp in the living room. She tried to see if she could get a better view. Nothing at all.

"Go away! I will call the police again!" Kinsey screamed at the top of her lungs. Minutes went by, but there was not another sound or knock. She was so frightened she could not get any sleep.

Angela Parker Jones

Kinsey noticed that there was blood on her living room floor, so she got a bucket, filled it with water and a cap full of Clorox, and began to clean her blood up. After she cleaned up the blood, Kinsey got in the shower and changed her clothes. At around 6:00 a.m., Kinsey finally fell asleep on her couch.

Hours later, Kinsey woke up. "Oh my!" said Kinsey. "It is so late!" It was three fifteen in the afternoon when she woke up. "I need to get myself together so I can go to the market," Kinsey said to herself.

She took a shower. After her shower, she dried herself. Kinsey was sore from the cut in her arm and leg, so she put on the most comfortable clothes she had in her closest—black yoga pants and an oversize white T-shirt. Kinsey looked all over for her red tennis shoes; she finally found them under her bed. After she put on her shoes, she put her hair into a high ponytail.

Makeup, Kinsey thought to herself. She put on red lipstick to match her shoes. Kinsey grabbed her purse, and out the door she went. She got into her car and locked the doors. She just sat

Angela Parker Jones

there for a minute or two and looked around her neighborhood. Kinsey saying to herself, "Why would someone want to hurt me?"

She drove off to the market. Turning off her engine, Kinsey walked into the market and grabbed a shopping cart. As she walked through the aisles, she greeted everyone with a smile and told them, "Good afternoon."

As Kinsey looked down and grabbed her calculator, a voice behind her spoke, "Hello, beautiful." It was a creepy, deep voice.

Kinsey turned around, slightly smiling. "Hi. Thank you," Kinsey said with a startled voice.

"My name is Rodger, and yours?"

"My name is Kinsey," she said, a perplexed look on her face.

"I just wanted to let you know that I think you are the most beautiful woman I've ever seen," Rodger said, smiling and walking away, still keeping his eyes on Kinsey.

"Thank you," Kinsey said, smiling slightly and turning away.

Angela Parker Jones

After picking up a few more items, Kinsey made her way to the cash register. As she was checking out, Kinsey looked around for Rodger. He was nowhere to be found. Kinsey walked to her car, looking around as she put her groceries in her trunk.

When Kinsey got in her car, she saw she had a missed call from Sarah. She sent a quick text to Sarah, telling her that she was okay and she was on her way back home.

About three miles down the street, a man came out of nowhere and jumped in front of Kinsey's car.

Boom!

Kinsey jumped out of the car to see if the man was okay. "Sir, are you okay? OMG, you're bleeding everywhere!"

He did not respond. He just looked at her, trembling and gushing blood.

"Sir, stay down. I'm calling 911," Kinsey said, crying and panicking.

Angela Parker Jones

"Hello, 911, what's your emergency?"

"I need help! I hit a man, and he's hurt really bad. Please hurry!"

"Okay, ma'am, calm down. What's the address?"

"I'm about three miles down from the market on Parker Avenue."

"Okay, ma'am, I'm sending help now."

Kinsey ended the phone call. She went back to the front of the car, where the man was, and he was gone!

"Where are you, sir! Sir, Where are you!" Kinsey ran back to the car to call 911, but it was too late. The firetruck and the ambulance had arrived.

The rescue team came running to Kinsey. "Where is he, ma'am?"

She was so frightened that she could barely speak. "He's . . . gone!"

The rescue team looked at one another, puzzled. "Look here, ma'am, we deal with hundreds of emergencies every day. We can't afford to respond to a little prank."

Kinsey looked mortified. "No, sir, you don't understand. I hit a man, and he was lying right here." Kinsey and the rescue men went back and forth, searching for the injured man, until the police arrived.

"Hello, ma'am, I'm Sergeant Pamala, and this is Sergeant Peter," said one of the two officers, introducing herself and her collegue.

"Hello, I'm Kinsey," she said with a raspy voice from the crying she'd been doing.

"First off, are you okay, Ms. Kinsey?" Sergeant Pamala said.

"No, I'm not okay, Sergeant! I hit a man, called for help, comes back, and he's gone without a trace in sight," Kinsey said, taking a seat on the sidewalk, holding her head down. "I just don't understand."

"Well, Ms. Kinsey, take it easy. How long has the man been gone?" said Sergeant Peter.

"About ten minutes."

"What about height, weight, hair color, age, clothes?"

"I would say late fifties or midsixties. He had frizzy dark-brown hair. His clothes were baggy and dingy," Kinsey said, looking at the spot she last saw the man.

"Thank you, Ms. Kinsey," Sergeant Peter said, taking his last few notes.

"Should we start a search for this man?" Sergeant Pamala asked Sergeant Peter.

"Call it in, Sergeant, and call in for backup. Ms. Kinsey, I need you to go with Sergeant Pamala to the station for further questions," said Sergeant Peter.

Kinsey and Sergeant Pamala got into the car and drove to the police station. When they arrived, Sergeant Pamala told Kinsey to sit in the interrogation room.

"Ms. Kinsey, please have a seat. I have to ask you a few more questions and write a report," Sergeant Pamala said, taking out her notebook. "Can you tell me why you didn't see the man before hitting him?"

"I don't know. I wasn't paying attention, and he just came out of nowhere," Kinsey said with tears flowing down her cheeks.

Angela Parker Jones

Sergeant Pam, looking sorry for her, as she wrote her comments down. She continued to ask more questions for about thirty minutes. After the questioning was over, Kinsey asked if she could leave.

"If we have any more questions, we will give you a call," Sergeant Pamala said, walking Kinsey to the door. "I'm so sorry you are going through this once again. If you need anything, you have my number."

"Thank you so much! Could I use your phone? I left my phone in my car. I need to call for a ride to get home," Kinsey asked.

"Of course, you can use my phone. But I'm about to leave out, and I'm going in the direction of your house. I can take you home," Sergeant Pamala said, putting on her coat.

"I would greatly appreciate it." Kinsey smiled. "I need to go get my groceries from my car if you do not mind?"

"Okay, we can stop at your car. Let me make a call, and we will meet at my car. I'm parked out front," Sergeant Pamala said, grabbing her cell phone. Kinsey headed towards Sergeant Pamala's car. "Hello, Sergeant Peter. "What's your location?"

"We are about to wrap up over here on Parker Avenue."

"Ms. Kinsey and I are on our way to the location," Sergeant Pam said, walking to her car. On their way there, Sergeant Pam asked Kinsey, "Ms. Kinsey, are you from around here?"

"I've lived here for about fifteen years. Am I still in questioning?" Kinsey said with sarcasm.

"Oh no, Ms. Kinsey, I'm just holding a general conversation. Hope I didn't intrude," Sergeant Pamala said while making a sharp turn, making Kinsey and her lean to the right a little.

"No, you didn't, Pamala. I was only joking. But like I said, I lived here for about fifteen years. I don't have much family here. Married once," Kinsey said, looking out the window.

"May I ask what happened to him?"

"Who? My husband? He was murdered."

"Oh, I'm so sorry to hear that," said Sergeant Pam.

"It's okay. The upsetting thing about his case was, they never found out who murdered him so they closed the case."

"How long was the case open?" Sergeant Pamala said, raising an eyebrow.

"Well . . ." Kinsey paused for a minute. "The case was only open for three months. It's like they barely did anything. I guess his death didn't matter to them," Kinsey said with a quiver in her voice.

"Oh, Ms. Kinsey," Sergeant Pamala said, glancing at Kinsey. "Would you like for us to end this conversation? I'm so sorry to startle you with bringing this up."

"Oh, sweetie, it's fine. Sometimes I just wonder what happened, why and who did it," Kinsey said.

"If you like, I could do a little research to see what I can find out."

"Oh no, no, Sergeant Pam!"

"I understand. I do not want to upset you! You're already going through enough," Sergeant Pamala said with a baffled face.

As they pulled into the crime scene, Kinsey had her head turned toward the window, gazing in deep thought.

"Ms. Kinsey, we are here!"

As they began to walk toward her car, Kinsey looked at all the yellow crime scene tape marking off the scene. As she was walking, she grabbed her groceries and personal things out of her car and placed them in Sergeant Pam's car.

"Is that everything?"

"Yes, I have everything."

"Let's roll!" Sergeant Pam said. "We are going to have to ask you further questions later, but in the meantime, you get some rest."

"Thanks for your concern, Sergeant Pam."

As Sergeant Pam was driving, Kinsey began gazing out her passenger window again. "I really appreciate all the help you guys are doing for me," said Kinsey.

"No problem. That's what we are here for, Ms. Kinsey," Sergeant Pamala said. She was getting closer to Kinsey's neighborhood, and she turned on to 0640 York Road. "All righty, Ms. Kinsey, we are here."

"Thank you, Sergeant Pam."

Sergeant Pam unlocked her car door so that Kinsey could get out. As Kinsey got out, she paused for a moment and looked around before grabbing her groceries.

"Do you need help?" Sergeant Pamala asked.

"Yes, please," Kinsey said, grabbing as many bags as her one arm would let her. Kinsey walked toward her door to unlock it.

The door was not locked.

"Why is my door unlocked?" Kinsey said with a startled voice.

Sergeant Pam grabbed her groceries out of the car but sat them by the door. "Ms. Kinsey, please step back!" She pulled out her gun and pushed the door open slowly. "This is the police. Come out with your hands up!"

Sergeant Pam walked in slowly. She walked from the living room and looked into the kitchen, bedroom, bathrooms, dining area, and living room. She then looked out the back door, but there was no one there.

"Ms. Kinsey, you can come in now."

Kinsey walked in slowly.

"Ms. Kinsey, I didn't see anything. Are you sure you didn't leave your door unlocked?" Sergeant Pamala said with a firm voice.

"Yes, I'm sure. I always lock my door. I just don't understand what's going on," said Kinsey.

Sergeant Pamala got an emergency call from the station. "I must leave now. Please, Ms. Kinsey, get some rest," Sergeant Pamala said.

"I will try. And thank you so much. One more thing, when will I know something about my car?"

"I don't know as of right now, Ms. Kinsey. Hopefully soon." Sergeant Pam walked out and looked back. "Please do not—and I repeat, *do not*—hesitate to call me or Sergeant Peter if you need anything."

"Okay, I will make sure I keep that in mind."

Sergeant Pam got in her car and backed out of the driveway then pulled off. Kinsey locked her door then headed to the kitchen to put her groceries away. After she put them all away, she then headed to the bathroom to take a hot shower. Kinsey turned on her water and grabbed her nightgown from the bedroom to bring in the bathroom.

She then undressed to get in the shower. Kinsey spent about fifteen minutes in her shower. When she was finished, she grabbed her towel to dry off. When she finished drying, she grabbed her nightgown, and a note fell to the floor. She picked up the note.

The note said, "You will be next to die!"

Kinsey dropped the note, screaming and backing toward her wall. Too scared to move, she screamed out loud, "Please leave me alone! Please!" But no one answered.

Angela Parker Jones

Kinsey, trembling, tried to get to her phone on the nightstand. She finally made it to her phone and picked it up. No dial tone. She then pushed the receiver down several times. Still nothing.

Kinsey really started to panic. "Who are you!" No one answered again.

Suddenly, she heard someone walking in another room. Tears started racing down her face. The footsteps lead to her front door. The door opened and slammed shut. Kinsey was afraid to move because she didn't know if the person had left or not. She doesn't know if the person left or not.

Kinsey looked around for a weapon. She took the lampshade and grabbed the base of it. It was about two feet tall and a half inch wide. Kinsey backed into a corner where no one could see her. Kinsey began crying and trembling as she listened for sounds.

The phone rang. *Ring, ring, ring!*

Kinsey quickly turned her head toward the phone, looking bewildered as to why it was ringing.

The ring stopped. Then a couple seconds later, it rang again. *Ring! Ring! Ring!*

Kinsey moved slowly toward the phone. "H-hell-lo . . ." said Kinsey, clearing her throat. No one said a word. "Who are you? What do you want?" Kinsey said, weeping. Still, no one said a word. Kinsey hung up the phone, but she didn't call the police this time.

She mumbled under her breath. "I will take this matter into my own hands."

Kinsey began to move slowly toward the kitchen. She grabbed her gloves off the countertop. Then she grabbed the knife. Then she looked into a drawer in the kitchen and found some duct tape. She began to wrap the tape around the knife. She began to turn off the lights.

She screamed at the top of her lungs, "Come on! Come on right now, you bastard! I know you are here!" No one came or responded.

About twenty minutes later she had a knock at her door. *Knock, knock, knock!*

Kinsey moved slowly to the door. "Who is it?"

Angela Parker Jones

No one answered.

"I said, who is it?"

Still, no one answered.

She had her knife behind her back as she slowly opened the door. Out of nowhere, a body fell into her front door.

Kinsey screamed, "Sarah! Sarah! Are you okay? Who did this to you?"

Sarah did not answer, bleeding to death. Kinsey screamed and shook Sarah to bring her back to consciousness. Still no response. Kinsey checked to see if Sarah was breathing. She was dead! Kinsey passed out.

When Kinsey woke up, Sarah was not there. She walked to Sarah's house and knocked at the door. Sarah did not come to the door. Kinsey went back home and tried calling Sarah on the phone.

Ring, ring, ring! There was no answer.

Kinsey called the police. Sergeant Peter picked up. "Sergeant Peter. May I help you?"

"Hello, Sergeant Peter, this is Kinsey. Can you please come? My neighbor is in trouble! I think she is dead!"

"I will be right there, Ms. Kinsey."

Later, Sergeant Peter and Sergeant Pam arrived at Sarah's house.

Kinsey came out to meet them both. "Hello, you guys," she said with a startled voice. "I feel my friend Sarah is in great danger. I think she is dead!

"Why would you think she is dead, Ms. Kinsey?" said Sergeant Pam.

"I had a crazy night last night. Someone knocked at my door. I opened the door and Sarah fell into my door and she was not breathing! I don't know what happened after that. When I woke up, I was lying on the floor, and Sarah was no longer there. When I opened the door, someone pushed her into my house. I did not see who it was. Now I can't find my friend. I need for you both to see if she is in her house, please!"

Angela Parker Jones

Sergeant Pam and Sergeant Peter started walking toward Sarah's door and tried calling out to her, but there was no answer. They began to knock. No answer.

Sergeant Pam and Sergeant Peter looked at each other, saying, "We got to go in." They both pulled out their guns.

Sergeant Peter said, "We are coming in!" He shot the lock on the door handle. The door opened. "We are coming in!" He said, going in first, moving slowly. Sergeant Pam went in behind him. Kinsey started to walk behind Sergeant Pam.

"No! Stay back, Ms. Kinsey," said Sergeant Pam.

They began walking toward Sarah's kitchen with both their backs to each other, looking around. No Sarah.

"Ms. Sarah, are you here?" Sergeant Peter walked into the bathroom. Still no Sarah. They walked into the living room. The TV was on, but no Sarah.

"Ms. Sarah! Are you here?" No answer.

They went to the bedroom. No Sarah. The bed was made up. There were no signs of her recently lying down in her bed. Sergeant Pam and Sergeant Peter checked her backyard. Still no Sarah.

"I wonder where Ms. Sarah is," said Sergeant Peter. He wonders whether it was worth the risk.

Sergeant Pam said, "She has to be close or in the neighborhood. She left the TV on, and her keys are here."

"You are right. But where could she be?" said Sergeant Peter.

They both went back in and walked out to the front door.

Kinsey said, "Is she there?"

"I'm afraid not," replied Sergeant Pam.

Kinsey said, "Someone's got her!"

"Calm down, Ms. Kinsey. We have to do a search in the neighborhood." Sergeant Pam looked puzzled. "Ms. Kinsey, can we take a look at your front door?"

"Sure," said Kinsey.

Sergeant Pam and Sergeant Peter walked next door. They did an inspection for evidence.

Sergeant Pam said, "I'm surprised I don't see any blood or anything! We have to do a search in the neighborhood. Ms. Kinsey, I will call you if we have any questions."

"Okay, I will be right here. I hope you guys find my friend!"

Sergeant Pam and Sergeant Peter said, "We will do our best. We have to go now."

Kinsey went back into her home with tears rolling down her face. She began to talk to herself, "What happened to my dear friend?" Tears ran down her face.

Meanwhile, Sergeant Peter and Sergeant Pam began going from house to house. No luck. They rode around for about two hours in the neighborhood.

Sergeant Peter said, "Let's head back to the station."

As they were leaving the neighborhood, Sergeant Pam had a bewildered look on her face.

Angela Parker Jones

"Are you okay Sergeant Pam?"

Speaking slowly, Sergeant Pam said, "Yes. I need you to drop me off at the station. I am going to head back to Ms. Kinsey's house. I have to ask her a few more questions."

"Do you need me to go back with you?" said Sergeant Peter asked.

"No, I can handle this. You go head to your family. It has been a long day."

Sergeant Peter looked at Sergeant Pam. "Okay, if you say so. If you need me, call me no matter what time it is, Sergeant Pam."

"Okay, I will. Don't worry," she said with a smile on her face.

Once they got to the station, they got out of the police car. Sergeant Peter went back into the station. Sergeant Pam got into her car. She began to head back to Kinsey's house. She called Kinsey on the phone. No answer.

Sergeant Pam continued driving to Kinsey's home. She finally arrived at Kinsey's home.

Angela Parker Jones

As Sergeant Pam arrived, she drove into the driveway, slowly staring at the house. She stepped out of her car and headed to Kinsey's front door and knocked a few times.

"Ms. Kinsey! It is Sergeant Pam. Ms. Kinsey! Can you hear me?" No answer.

Sergeant Pam began walking toward the back of the house. There were no signs of Kinsey. She began moving slowly to the back. As she took a step up toward the door, she noticed a hump on the ground to the far left of Kinsey's fence. As she was knocking on the door, she stared again.

Finally, Kinsey opened the door with a smile. "Hello, Sergeant Pam, may I ask why are you here again?"

Sergeant Pam looked puzzled, wondering why Kinsey opened the door with a smile on her face. "Well, I have a question. When Ms. Sarah fell into your door, did she have any blood on her?"

"Yes," Kinsey said.

"Well, my next question is," Sergeant Pamala said, looking confused, "then who cleaned the blood up?"

Kinsey said, "I don't know."

Sergeant Pam said, "Who has the time as a killer to clean up any blood? And another thing. Why would you open the door, knowing that no one answered?"

Kinsey became angry. She suddenly pulled Sergeant Pam into her house, choking her.

Sergeant Pam gasped for breath. "Let me go!"

"No, you will die today. You should not have come back here, snooping and questioning me," said Kinsey.

Sergeant Pam and Kinsey struggled for a while. As Sergeant Pam began to pull her gun out, Kinsey stabbed her in her neck. Sergeant Pam died instantly. She dropped to the floor.

Looking enraged, Kinsey said, "You deserved to die!"

Sergeant Pam lay on the floor, bleeding to death.

It was getting late in the evening. Kinsey went into her bathroom to get the items to clean up the blood from Sergeant Pam. When she came back into her kitchen, Sergeant Pam was gone, and so was the blood. Kinsey looked out the window, and Sergeant Pamala's car was gone. Kinsey panicked!

She looked around for her. She started screaming, "Where are you, Sergeant Pam? I know I killed you!"

Suddenly, a door slammed shut. She ran to look; it was her back door. The curtains were still moving. She ran outside; no one was there. Kinsey came back inside. Breathing heavily, Kinsey looked puzzled and was panicking. As she walked toward her bedroom, there was a knock at the door.

It was Sergeant Peter. He screamed, "It's Sergeant Peter, Ms. Kinsey!"

"Oh my, what am I going to do?" said Kinsey.

Sergeant Peter knocked again. "Ms. Kinsey, are you home?"

Kinsey walked in circles several times. She finally pulled herself together and approached the door. She looked out her peephole, and Sergeant Peter was still there, looking at the door from the other side.

She finally opened the door. "Yes, Sergeant Peter?" said Kinsey.

"Ms. Kinsey, I'm going to have to ask you to come to the police station for questioning."

"But why, Sergeant Peter?"

"We got a call that Sergeant Pam was found dead in a park, covered with a blanket."

"Well, what does that have to do with me?" said Kinsey.

"I do know that Sergeant Pam told me she was going to see you before she went home. So I will ask you one more time to come with me please."

Kinsey held her arms out so that Sergeant Peter could cuff her. Sergeant Peter walked her to the car. Kinsey's head hit the top of the car while getting in.

"Ouch!" screamed Kinsey.

"Be careful, Ms. Kinsey."

Kinsey slid to the middle of the back seat of the police car. They then drove off. Once they arrived to the police station, Sergeant Peter got out and opened Kinsey's door. As Sergeant Peter opened Kinsey's door, he told her to be careful getting out.

Once they entered the police station, Sergeant Peter asked Kinsey to enter a room with nothing but a table and four chairs. It was the interrogating room.

"Why am I in a room with nothing in it?" said Kinsey.

Sergeant Peter replied, "Well, Ms. Kinsey, like I said, I have some questions for you. First, I want to run some things by you that I took notice of since I met you."

"Okay," Kinsey said with her head down.

"Ms. Kinsey, first, you called us because someone broke into your house and tried to kill you and got away. Second, you hit a man, but when we got there, there were no signs he was there. Third, your neighbor was killed and fell

Angela Parker Jones

into your house. When you woke up, Ms. Sarah was not there. And finally, Sergeant Pam went to your house, but she did not return home or give me a call to let me know if she was safe. My question is, do you have any clue what's going on, Ms. Kinsey?"

"No, I don't!"

"So you have no clue what happened to everyone?"

"I told you no, Sergeant Peter!"

"Ms. Kinsey, I did some research. I have a folder in here with all your information."

"What information, Sergeant Peter?"

"Ms. Kinsey, I am afraid you have to go back to the mental institution. You have a history of doing evil things and not remembering what you did."

"No, I will not go back! I am fine, Sergeant Peter." Kinsey was panicking. "I take my medication. It is someone out there doing this, and it is not me!" Kinsey said, crying. "Please don't do this me!"

"I'm afraid, Ms. Kinsey, you must go back. I am so sorry."

Kinsey was screaming and kicking. "No! Please don't!"

Sergeant Peter and a few more officers escorted Kinsey to the car to take her to Randolph Mental Institution.

Once they arrived at the institution, they had to put Kinsey in a straitjacket because she wouldn't calm down. They signed her in, and the doctors gave her pills to calm her down.

After, Kinsey calmed down. A nurse came in to escort Kinsey to Doctor Cunningham's office.

"Ms. Kinsey, tell me what's going on," said Doctor Cunningham.

"I don't feel comfortable," Kinsey said, sitting up in her chair. "I don't understand why Sergeant Peter would send me here."

"Well, Ms. Kinsey, he feels like you need someone to talk to. I'm here to listen," said Doctor Cunningham. "How about we start off by introducing ourselves?"

"That would be great," said Kinsey, slightly smiling.

"I'm Doctor Victoria Cunningham. I've been a psychiatrist for over four years now."

"Hello, Doctor Cunningham. I'm Kinsey Miller. I've lived here in Merry Hill, North Carolina, for about fifteen years. I moved here with my husband. I enjoy painting pictures and writing," said Kinsey, pushing her glasses up from her nose. "Do you want to know more?"

"No, Ms. Kinsey, that is fine for now," Doctor Cunningham said, grabbing her notebook. "You said you moved here with your husband. What was his name?"

"His name was Archie Miller."

"How was your relationship?"

"Well, my husband was murdered a year ago in our home," Kinsey said, looking everywhere but in Doctor Cunningham's face.

"I'm so sorry to hear that. How are you holding up?" Doctor Cunningham said, writing in her notebook.

"I'm taking it a day at a time. It doesn't bother me as much as it did the day I found out, so that's a good thing, right?"

"That's great," Doctor Cunningham said, writing more notes in her notebook. "Would you tell me about the things that's been going on recently?"

"A few weeks ago, someone broke into my home, trying to kill me, I believe."

"Why would someone want to kill you, Ms. Kinsey?"

"I don't know. I wish I know," said Kinsey, beginning to cry.

"Take it easy, Ms. Kinsey. Do you know who or why someone killed your husband?"

"My husband was a kind man, very loving and thoughtful. He was a successful man. He owned a computer software company," Kinsey said, smiling slightly. "I loved him."

"What a man," Doctor Cunningham said, holding Kinsey's hand because she began to cry again, harder this. "Ms. Kinsey, I think we did enough today." Doctor Cunningham closed her

Angela Parker Jones

notebook. "I want to see you tomorrow. Sergeant

Peter is really worried about your mental state,

so I need to test you on a few things."

"Okay, Doctor Cunningham. Thank you for

meeting with me today," Kinsey said.

"No, thank you," Doctor Cunningham said,

helping Kinsey out of her office. After Kinsey

left Doctor Cunningham's office, she called

Sergeant Peter.

"Hello, this Sergeant Peter."

"Hello, Sergeant Peter, this is Mrs. Cunningham. I wanted to talk to you about Ms. Kinsey."

"I'm listening."

"Did you know her husband was murdered inside their home about a year ago?"

"No. She never told me that."

"His name was Archie Miller. He owned a computer software company," Doctor Cunningham said, looking over her notes that she took with Kinsey. "I'm meeting with her tomorrow to take a few tests with her."

"Please e-mail me the results," Sergeant Peter said, ending the phone call.

After Kinsey got back in her room, a nurse came in and gave her some medicine. Kinsey went straight to sleep. Four hours later, she woke up, and there was a man sitting in a dark corner. She was still kind of out of it, so her vision was blurry. She closed her eyes and opened them back up.

"Who are you?" Kinsey said.

The man just laughed. "Ha ha ha!" He had a deep, wicked voice. He had a very deeply baritone voice. The man replied, "You still have not recognized who I am?"

"No," said Kinsey. "Who are you?"

He stood up and came forward enough where the light could hit him in the face.

Kinsey screamed, "Archie! I thought you were dead!"

"No, you thought you killed me! You left me in the woods to die! Now it's time for you to suffer!" Archie laughed. "All those killings they thought you did, I was the one who took everyone from the scene. I killed Sarah," Archie said, walking toward Kinsey's bed. "I buried everyone in your backyard, by the fence. So when they search your property and find them, you will never leave this mental institution as long as I'm around!"

Kinsey blanked out.

Made in the USA
Columbia, SC
01 February 2018